Merlin

This series is for my riding friend
Shelley, who cares about all animals.

STRIPES PUBLISHING
An imprint of Magi Publications
1 The Coda Centre, 189 Munster Road, London SW6 6AW

A paperback original
First published in Great Britain in 2007

Text copyright © Jenny Oldfield, 2007
Illustrations copyright © Sharon Rentta, 2007
Cover illustration © Simon Mendez, 2007

ISBN-13: 978-1-84715-035-6

A CIP catalogue record for this book is available from the British Library.

Printed and bound in China

2 4 6 8 10 9 7 5 3 1

Merlin

Tina Nolan
Illustrated by Sharon Rentta

ANIMAL MAGIC
Meet the animals

Visit our website at
www.animalmagicrescue.net

Working our
magic to match
the perfect pet
with the perfect
owner!

BRUNO
A golden Labrador,
about four years old.
Bruno is a lovely dog
who likes people.

LOTTIE
This 2-year-old cairn
terrier is a bundle of fun!
Lottie loves children and
would like to come
out to play!

JOEY
Joey the greyhound is
too old to race. He
would love a comfy,
quiet home where he
can dream of rabbits!

RESCUE CENTRE
in need of a home!

GUINEVERE AND MERLIN
Mother and foal require
rehoming together.
Guinevere hacks out in
company and alone at all
paces. Good in traffic.

DOUGAL
An active and energetic
Dalmatian with bags of
character. Can you keep
up with this playful chap?

SUGAR AND SPICE
Sugar and Spice are
orphans. They're ready
to go to new owners
and would like
a home together.

SAGE AND THYME
Two more orphan kittens
are looking for a friendly
new home. Can you
step in and give them
the love they need?

Chapter One

"Almost there!" Eva called to her brother, Karl.

Karl was climbing a tree to rescue Tigger, a tabby cat who had managed to get himself stuck.

"Climb to your right – a bit further," Eva instructed. "Yes, now try!"

Karl eased himself along a branch close to Tigger. He reached out with one hand.

"Take care!" Tigger's owner, Miss Eliot,

warned. She held her hands to her mouth, hardly daring to look.

"That's it, you're nearly there." Jimmy Harrison, Karl and Eva's grandfather, urged his grandson on.

The cat cowered on a branch. His yellow eyes glinted.

"Come here, Tigger!" Karl called softly.

He stretched as far as he dared.

Down below, Eva, their grandad and Miss Eliot watched anxiously.

"Don't you worry," Jimmy told Miss Eliot. "We'll soon have Tigger down."

"That's good," Karl whispered as the cat stretched out a paw. "Come on, Tigger."

Tigger inched forward, his tail between his legs. Finally, Karl reached out and took hold of him.

"Cool!" Eva cried, as Karl clasped the cat to him and began to climb down.

"Oh my!" Miss Eliot gasped, smiling with relief.

Jimmy Harrison grinned at his elderly neighbour. "I told you Karl could do it! Now all you have to do is open up a can of food and give him his supper. And while you're at it you can put the kettle on for a nice cup of tea!"

As their grandad and the old lady disappeared inside the big house, Eva welcomed Karl and Tigger back to earth.

"Nice one!" she grinned at her brother, taking the cat from him while he brushed himself down.

"Animal Magic at your service, ma'am!" he laughed.

"Yeah, whatever. Anyway, I'm glad Grandad thought to ring us. Miss Eliot was about to call the fire brigade!"

"Hmmm... It's a good job Grandad lives next door," Karl muttered. Looking up at Miss Eliot's big house, Karl could see paint peeling from the window frames and ivy choking the broken gutters. "Ash Tree Manor is one gigantic house for an old lady living by herself."

Eva nodded, then carried Tigger indoors. "Who's hungry?" she murmured.

The second he saw his food dish, Tigger leaped clear. Soon he was munching happily.

"Thank you so much," Miss Eliot told Eva and Karl. "It's a relief to have Tigger back safe and sound."

Eva and Karl blushed. Their grandad smiled proudly.

"Now I know why your rescue centre is called Animal Magic," the old lady said, shedding a happy tear. "It's as if I waved a magic wand and you brought Tigger and me a happy ending. We simply can't thank you enough!"

"OK, Bruno, lie still while I have a look at you." Heidi Harrison spoke gently to the golden Labrador on her examination table.

Eva and Karl had raced back from Ash Tree Manor and burst in on their mum's surgery, eager to tell her the exciting Tigger rescue story.

The injured dog whimpered and stared up at Heidi with his deep brown eyes.

Joel Allerton, Heidi's assistant, stood close by. "Slow down," he said. "This poor chap's had a nasty fall. He was found at the foot of a seven-metre high wall. It looks like he's torn a ligament."

Carefully Heidi tested the movement in Bruno's shoulder joint. "Yes," she confirmed. "He's probably going to need keyhole surgery to fix it."

"What happened? Did somebody dump him?" Eva asked.

Joel nodded.

"Your dad found him on the outskirts of town, where the railway bridge crosses the road. We think he got pushed over the edge and landed on the grass verge."

"And will he be OK?" Suddenly their exciting story about rescuing Tigger didn't seem half so important.

Her mum nodded. "He should be fine. He's been very lucky. There's a name tag on his collar, but no phone number. He's not microchipped either, so it'll be hard to trace the owner."

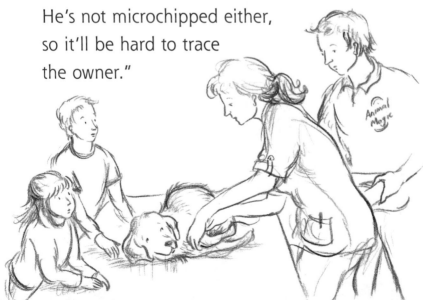

"Poor Bruno!" Eva murmured. Inside, she boiled with anger over the idea that anyone could shove this beautiful dog off a bridge. She stood back as Joel prepared a painkilling injection.

The dog whimpered again and raised his head.

Karl frowned. "Can I enter him on the website?" he asked.

"Go ahead, put his details up," Heidi said. She took the syringe from Joel and stroked Bruno's ears. "'Golden Lab, male, about four years old. A lovely dog who likes people.'"

Nodding, Karl disappeared into the office and sat at the computer. He typed quickly then came back to take a photo of Bruno to put on the site.

"Where's Dad?" Eva asked.

"Outside, putting the finishing touches

to the stables," her mum told her. "Can't you hear him hammering?"

Yes, the stables! The very word cheered Eva up.

Animal Magic was about to open its doors to bigger unwanted animals such as horses, ponies and goats, as well as the dogs, cats and rabbits they already looked after. A team of volunteers had given up their time to convert a cowshed in the corner of the old farmyard. By this time next week the stables would be ready.

"I'll go and help!" she decided, escaping from the surgery and across the yard to join her dad.

Chapter Two

All that evening and the next day, Eva worked in the new stables with her dad. She used a screwdriver to fix bolts on doors, and a hammer to nail planks of wood to a partition wall.

"Good job," her dad told her before he left for work the following morning. "Tonight I'll pick up the bales of straw I ordered from Tom Ingleby's farm. You can come with me if you like."

"Yes please." Eva always enjoyed a visit

to Tom's place. High Trees Farm was on the edge of the village and Tom owned the fields at the back of Animal Magic.

Eva hammered on. "How's Bruno?" she asked Joel when he popped his head over the stable door.

"Surgery went well," Joel replied. "The shoulder should heal within a few days."

"That's great news." Eva knew that Karl had already taken two enquiries about Bruno on the website. "At this rate, we'll get him better and find him a new home before the end of the half-term holiday."

"Another success story," Joel grinned. "We're working our magic..."

"...to match the perfect pet..."

"...with the perfect owner!" Joel and Eva chanted the Animal Magic slogan.

Eva put down her hammer and stood back. "Time for a break," she decided.

"Fancy coming to pick up our bulk order of cat food from the Red Barn?" Joel asked.

"Yes, cool. I'll just let Mum know." She followed him out to the yard, trying to creep past Mrs Brooks next door without attracting attention.

But Linda Brooks looked up from planting a neat row of red and white flowers along the side of her lawn.

"How's Annie getting on in Devon?" Eva asked about her friend who was on holiday with her cousins.

"Fine thank you, Eva," came the brisk reply. Mrs Brooks peeled off her gardening gloves and came up to the wall. "Joel, I'd like a word with you if you can spare a moment!"

"Sure. What can I do for you, Linda?"

"You can pass on a message, please. I'd like you to tell Heidi to expect a visit from the Council."

Joel and Eva exchanged worried looks.

"Jason and I have lodged our petition at the Town Hall," Mrs Brooks explained. "We gathered signatures of people opposing Animal Magic on the grounds of excess animal noise and car traffic, and I delivered the petition to the Council office on Monday morning."

"Good for you, Linda," Joel muttered under his breath.

Eva could hardly bear to listen. *This is the countryside!* she thought. *Animals live in the country. You expect them to make noise!* She couldn't believe that Annie's parents had actually gone ahead and done what they'd been threatening to do ever since Animal Magic started up a year earlier.

"So you'll inform Heidi?" Linda asked stiffly. Joel nodded. Mrs Brooks gave a triumphant smile before turning on her heel and going back to her gardening.

Joel sighed and hung his head. "Come on, Eva, let's forget the cat food," he muttered. "I'd better pass this news on to your mum before I lose control and leap over that fence to tear up Linda's precious flower bed!"

"I've been expecting it," Heidi admitted when Eva and Joel gave her Mrs Brooks's message. She was in her surgery, busy with a new arrival – a cat which was still fastened inside a wicker basket, miaowing to be let out.

"Mrs Brooks is so mean!" Eva cried. "She's asking the Council to close us down without even thinking about what will happen to all our animals if they do!"

"I know." Over the months Heidi had got used to her neighbour's constant complaints and threats. Even now she was determined not to let it upset her. "Let's not think about that now, Eva. Why don't you open up the basket and help me take a look at this little chap."

"What if Animal Magic has to close?" Eva demanded, unbuckling the leather strap. "Where will all our animals go?"

"Not now, Eva. Joel, we'll need to open a new bay in the cattery. Can you go and make sure there's food and water?" Eva opened the basket and Heidi reached inside, lifting out a wary tabby cat with staring yellow eyes.

"Hey, that's Tigger!" Eva recognized him straight away. She ran to the door and called for Karl, who was busy cleaning his bike in the yard. "Karl, come and look. Miss Eliot's tabby has been brought in!"

"What happened?" Karl asked, his forehead damp under his floppy, dark fringe. He'd just cycled to Okeham and back with his friend, George Stevens.

"Hey, Tigger!" Eva murmured, stroking his soft, striped fur. "What's happened to Miss Eliot?" she asked her mum.

"Better ask your grandad," Heidi answered, beginning to examine the new arrival. "He brought Tigger in half an hour ago."

"Let's cycle over there," Karl said in a hurry, hardly waiting for Eva to grab her bike and follow.

Eva and Karl pedalled hard along Main Street, towards their grandfather's garden

centre on the edge of Okeham. Soon
they saw the large green and white
Gro-Well sign and the long rows of
glasshouses where Jimmy Harrison grew
and sold his plants.

"Grandad, how come you brought
Tigger to the rescue centre?" Karl asked,
charging into the shop.

Eva was hard on his heels. "What happened to Miss Eliot? Is she OK?"

Jimmy, who was potting small green seedlings into larger pots, looked over the rim of his glasses. "Ah, yes. Not good news, I'm afraid," he murmured. "I found poor Miss Eliot collapsed on her kitchen floor this morning. I had to ring for an ambulance."

"Did she go to hospital?" Eva gasped.

Her grandad nodded. "I've no idea how long she'll be there, but she asked me to take care of her animals."

Karl fiddled with the plastic plant labels on the counter. "Animals – plural?"

"I thought Tigger was the only one," Eva cut in.

"Tigger is the only *cat*," her grandad agreed. "And it was easy enough for me to drop him off at your place."

"But?" Karl prompted.

"But Guinevere is more of a problem," Jimmy admitted. "I've already phoned your dad and he's coming over as soon as he can."

"Guinevere?" Eva stared at the tall, grey house next door. "Who's she?"

"Come and see," their grandad invited. He led the way down the side of the glasshouse and through a narrow gate into a field beyond. "I couldn't exactly fit this fine lady into the back of my Land Rover!"

The green field sloped gently towards a stream where a row of willow trees grew. As Eva and Karl took in their new surroundings, they made out a large, grey shape in the shadow of the overhanging branches.

"Wow, is that a pony?" Karl exclaimed.

Eva's mouth fell open. Sure enough, a beautiful dapple-grey pony emerged from the trees. Her mane and tail were pure white. She trod heavily up the hill towards them.

"Meet Guinevere," their grandad announced. "This is Miss Eliot's grey mare. And as you can see, she's about to give birth to a foal any day now!"

Chapter Three

"She's gorgeous!" Eva breathed, watching her dad and grandad begin to load the grey mare into a trailer which Mark had borrowed from Tom Ingleby.

Guinevere's mane was silky soft, and her dappled coat shone in the sunlight.

"Take good care of her," Jimmy Harrison said. "Remember, I promised Miss Eliot that her pony would get five star treatment!"

"Looks like we'll have to open the

stables early," Karl said. "Shall I go ahead and make sure everything's ready?"

His dad nodded. "I dropped off the bales of straw on the way here. Eva, you go with your brother and make a nice deep bed in the stable closest to the door, OK?"

As Karl rode off, Eva lingered to see her dad lead Guinevere safely up the ramp into the trailer. Then she set off, pedalling hard until she reached home.

"Mum," she yelled, "Dad's bringing a pony! She's having a foal! We have to lay straw in a stable for her!"

Heidi stood in the doorway to the surgery. "I know. Karl already told me. It's exciting, isn't it?"

"Totally. She's gorgeous, Mum. Just wait till you see her!" Flinging her bike down, Eva raced into the stable block, where she found Karl cutting through string that tied the bales of straw. She dived in and took an armful, scattering it on the floor. "How cool is this!"

"Calm down," Karl grunted. "Look at you – you're covered in straw."

"I don't care. We're getting a pony!" Eva's dark eyes shone. Suddenly she stared at Karl. "Hey, do you think the foal will be born while Guinevere's here?"

"It depends how long Miss Eliot has to stay in hospital," Karl pointed out.

"The pony did look pretty pregnant, didn't she?" Eva said eagerly.

"Oh, so now you're an expert, are you?" As usual, Karl tried not to let his feelings show.

"I bet she has the foal here!" Eva insisted. "How cool will that be?"

At the sound of their dad's van, they

both ran out into the yard. They helped him slide the bolts at the back of the trailer, and then lower the ramp.

"Let's take a look at the mother-to-be," Heidi said, coming forward to examine Guinevere before they unloaded her. "Oh yes, it's going to be any day now. Bring her out gently. Keep her nice and calm."

Eva held her breath as her dad led Guinevere down the ramp. "Her stable's ready," she said, holding the door open.

"Easy, girl," Mark said. He waited for the mare to take in her new surroundings.

She stood in the doorway, looking this way and that. Her ears were pricked and she swished her tail. Then she must have decided that her new home was good enough, because she stepped forward on to the fresh straw bed and let out a long, satisfied snicker.

"Guinevere needs peace and quiet,"
Heidi told Eva. "When a mare is about to
give birth, the last thing she wants is
people petting her and fussing."

"But how will we know when it's
happening?" Eva asked.

"We may not. It often happens in the
middle of the night, quite naturally,
without any help from us."

Eva nodded. "So we come out in the morning and the foal is here, already tottering about on its wobbly legs!" She pictured the magical moment.

"Fingers crossed," Heidi said. "So what I'm saying is, leave Guinevere alone for a while. How about taking a dog for a walk instead?"

Eva nodded and went to fetch Dougal from the kennels. As she went in she was greeted by a chorus of woofs and barks.

"Hey, Sam, hey, Lottie, hey, Millie," she said as she passed by each kennel, saying hello to a retriever, a cairn terrier and a cheeky cross-breed.

"Your turn for a walk, Dougal," she told the cute Dalmatian.

Dougal loved his runs along the river bank and when he saw the lead in Eva's hand he went crazy with delight.

"Down!" she told him sternly. "Heel!" she said as she got him on the lead.

They left the kennels, crossed the yard and went down an alley towards the river, where Eva let Dougal off the lead.

Off he dashed, sniffing at the entrance to a rabbit burrow, then on through the long grass with just the tip of his white tail showing.

"Dougal, come back!" Eva cried, as the playful Dalmatian made a sharp detour over a narrow stone bridge towards Okeham golf course.

Luckily he obeyed and came bounding back to Eva. Over the far side of the river, a group of golfers gathered on a smooth green. Eva recognized Jason Brooks, their next door neighbour.

"Heel, Dougal!" she murmured, glad that she and Karl had spent time training

him not to run off. He even ignored the
two fishermen sitting on the river bank,
who surprised Eva by standing up and
yelling at her to clear off.

Eva frowned. She didn't like the look of
the two men, who seemed to be angry
without good reason. "Come here,
Dougal. Heel!" she called again.

Obediently Dougal walked to heel, tail and head up, as they headed away from the river, along a footpath beside one of the fields belonging to Tom Ingleby. The footpath brought them back on to Main Street, where Eva put Dougal on the lead and walked him home. "Good boy!" she said with a grin, thinking that he looked like a pirate, with the big, black patch over one eye.

Dougal wagged his long tail and trotted into the kennels, where Eva settled him down for the night.

"Good night, Joey, good night, Trixie," she murmured, passing a greyhound and a Jack Russell.

The dogs yapped and wagged their tails. As Eva turned off the light and closed the door, they fell silent.

She crossed the yard and went into the

house, to find Karl at his computer, updating the Animal Magic website.

"Hi Eva. A woman is coming in to look at Dougal tomorrow," he reported.

"Cool. Where are Mum and Dad?"

"In their room."

Eva heard the low voices of her parents from across the landing. "The Council is sending someone to see us tomorrow afternoon," Heidi was saying. "They didn't give an exact time."

"Do you want me to be here?" Mark asked.

"No, there's no point. It's only a quick visit. I can tell them everything they need to know."

Eva gasped. "Did you hear that?" she hissed at Karl, who nodded.

"Let's hope they don't take Linda's side," Mark went on. "We could be in serious trouble if they do."

There was a long pause. "It will mean that all our work at Animal Magic will have to stop," Heidi admitted. "The Council could close us down overnight!"

Eva lay awake late that night worrying. Every time she closed her eyes she pictured a man from the Council signing a piece of paper saying that Animal Magic had to close.

Then who would find a home for Bruno once his shoulder had healed, or for Joey the greyhound who was too old to race any more? Who would look after animals like Tigger and Guinevere while their owners were in hospital?

Eva tossed and turned. It was no good – she couldn't sleep even if it was two o'clock in the morning! Getting out of bed, she crept to her window, opened it and listened to the silence. In the distance there was the low hoot of an owl.

I wonder how Guinevere is getting on? she thought, looking over at the stables. She listened in the darkness, and after a few moments was sure she could hear restless movements coming from the stables – the sound of the pony's feet rustling through dry straw, a low snort, the knock of a hoof against a wooden door. It was no good, whatever her mum had said about Guinevere needing peace and quiet, Eva had to go and take a look!

Chapter Four

Eva found Guinevere standing in her bed of straw. She tossed her head in the low glimmer of a safety lamp fixed high on the wall.

"Hey, girl!" Eva murmured. She watched anxiously as the mare began to pace to and fro, then folded her knees and went down on her side, only to get up and pace again. "Take it easy," Eva breathed.

But Guinevere was restless. She rustled

through the straw, went down again, rolled on to her other side and was back on her feet.

"I guess this is the time for your foal to be born," Eva whispered, feeling sure she was right. She didn't move.

Guinevere went down on her side a third time, and stayed. Her wide sides heaved as she laid her head on the straw.

"Oh!" Eva was scared. Guinevere looked agitated and helpless. Would it be OK to go right into the stall with her?

The mare lifted her head from the straw. She rolled her eyes.

"You're doing fine!" Eva murmured.

There were footsteps outside, and Heidi came into the stable. "I couldn't sleep either. I heard you come down," she muttered to Eva. She took one look at the mare. "Right, this is it!"

She went into the stable and knelt
down by Guinevere's side to test her
pulse. Then she held a stethoscope to the
mare's belly. "Uh-oh, the foal's heartbeat
isn't very strong. I think Guinevere will
need help to deliver it," she decided.
"Eva, Joel's on night duty. Run to the
surgery and fetch him."

Nodding, Eva ran off. She found Joel feeding a litter of orphan kittens with milk from plastic droppers. "Guinevere ... foal... Come quick!" she gasped.

Together they ran back to the stables.

"OK, this is happening quicker than I expected," Heidi warned. "The foal's head has already emerged. Joel help me ease it out. Eva, you stay where you are."

Anxiously Eva watched her mum and Joel assist Guinevere. She saw the new foal emerge and slither gently on to the straw.

"No panic, it's all over!" Heidi said, glancing up at Eva.

"Is she ... are *they* OK?" Eva asked.

Heidi's eyes were bright. "Come and see."

Eva tiptoed towards Guinevere's stall and peered in.

"I had to turn the foal's head and help him out," Heidi said. "He'd got himself jammed for a while back there."

Him? The foal was a "he"! Eva held her breath. And there he was – the smallest, youngest, skinniest, shakiest foal she'd ever seen!

The baby lay in the straw. His mother licked him clean, and then nudged him with her nose. He braced his front legs and tried to push himself up.

"His head is enormous!" Eva exclaimed. "And his legs are so skinny!"

Guinevere nudged and shoved him gently from behind. The foal was grey, like her, with big, dark eyes.

Once more he tried to stand. He got up and tottered, fell over, tried again.

"Aah!" Eva gasped. "How clever is that!"

"That's what they're programmed to do," Heidi told her quietly. "In the wild, they have to be up on their feet and running away from danger almost the minute they're born!"

And now the foal was standing on his shaky legs and Guinevere was licking him clean and he was turning to her and beginning to suckle.

"That is so-o-o magical!" Eva murmured. "Guinevere, you're amazing!"

"Would you like to give him a name?"

her mum asked, smiling at Joel.

Eva gazed at the suckling foal. "Let's call him Merlin," she whispered. "Like the wizard. 'Cos he's magic!"

"So, Miss Eliot, you'll be pleased to know that your mare has had her foal," Jimmy Harrison said.

He had brought Karl and Eva to visit the old lady in hospital just after lunch the following day. She looked pale and thin, propped up on pillows, with bedclothes folded neatly under her chin.

"He's grey, like his mum," Eva broke in. "His mane sticks straight up, and he's got the longest legs. I was there when he was born!"

"Slow down," Karl warned. "Sorry, Eva's always butting in."

Miss Eliot smiled weakly. "Not at all, you're excited, aren't you, dear? And so am I. I was looking forward to seeing the birth myself, but it wasn't to be."

"Merlin got up on his feet straight away!" Eva exclaimed.

"Merlin?" Miss Eliot interrupted.

Eva blushed. "Oh, Mum said I could give him a name – just for now – so I chose 'Merlin'."

"What a good choice. I think he should keep it. And how is my lovely Guinevere?"

"Mum says she's doing well," Karl reported. "And so is Tigger. He's happy in the cattery."

Miss Eliot nodded, and then turned her head towards Jimmy. "The doctors tell me I had a slight stroke – nothing too serious, but it's given me a shock."

"You'll have to take it easy from now on," Jimmy told her kindly. "When you get back home, I'll pop in and keep an eye on you, don't you worry."

Tears appeared in Miss Eliot's eyes. She shook her head and they trickled down her lined cheeks. "I'm afraid I won't be coming home, Mr Harrison."

"Well, not yet," he conceded. "But in a while, when you're stronger."

"Not ever," the old lady told him faintly. "I have to face facts and admit that Ash Tree Manor is too much for me now."

Jimmy was about to protest, but the old lady shook her head.

"I've lived in the old house all my life and I shall always have many wonderful memories of my time there. But now I've made up my mind to sell it and move into an apartment," Miss Eliot announced. "Tigger will be able to come with me, but not the ponies, of course."

Eva gasped in alarm. *This can't be happening!* she thought. She stared at the old lady's sad face.

"I would like your son and daughter-in-law to find a wonderful new home for Guinevere and her foal," Miss Eliot insisted. "I would be so grateful to them if they could succeed."

Chapter Five

"Guinevere and Merlin." Karl typed the ponies' names on to the Animal Magic website at the reception desk in the surgery. He remembered what Miss Eliot had told him. "Mother and foal need rehoming together. Guinevere hacks out in company and alone at all paces. Good in traffic. Merlin needs to be with his mum."

"Listen to this," Karl called out to Eva. "Does this sound OK?"

She listened carefully as he read out the new advert. "You've used two 'needs'," she pointed out.

"OK, Miss Fussy, I'll change the first 'need' to 'require'," Karl nodded then worked on. "I'll be out to take photos in a couple of minutes," he muttered. "Can you get Guinevere and Merlin ready?"

"How do you mean?" Eva asked.

"You know, brushing and grooming. Horsey stuff." Karl made out he didn't know or care much about it, but really he was as much in love with the mare and her foal as everyone else. Every time he looked at Merlin, his heart melted.

"Give me five minutes," Eva replied, dashing out to the stables. Once there, she slowed right down, moving quietly around the ponies as she mucked out and laid fresh straw, and then took a brush to Guinevere's long mane.

The mare stood patiently, keeping one watchful eye on her foal, who tottered unsteadily through the new straw.

"He's gorgeous, isn't he?" Eva murmured, smiling at Merlin's wobbly legs and soft, tufty tail. She couldn't believe how tiny his hooves were, or how big his eyes and ears seemed. And he wasn't scared of having her in the stall with them. Instead he came close and took a nip at the hem of Eva's T-shirt.

"Hey!" she protested with a smile. She turned and let him take a good sniff at her boots and jeans.

Then Guinevere nudged Eva from behind, as if to say, "You haven't finished yet." Eva turned back to Guinevere and was just giving her mane a final brush when someone opened the stable door.

"Nearly finished," she called out,
expecting Karl.

But it was her mum who interrupted.
"Eva, this is Mr Winters. He's come from
the Council to take a look at us."

Eva frowned and chewed her lip. In the
excitement of Merlin's birth, she'd
forgotten all about Linda Brooks's
petition and the visit from the Council.
She mumbled hello.

"We've just opened the stables," Heidi explained to their visitor. "Guinevere and Merlin are our first customers. I'm hoping to give shelter to goats, ponies and donkeys before finding them new owners. I also plan to link up with Leebank Pony Sanctuary to find a permanent place for those animals we can't rehome."

"So you don't intend to keep any large animals here long term?" Mr Winters checked. He was a small, stout man wearing a grey suit and a red and grey striped tie. He was carrying a blue folder and seemed to be making lots of notes.

Eva carried on grooming Guinevere as her mum led Mr Winters outside.

"No, but we do expect this section of the centre to be busy, just like the kennels and the cattery," Heidi answered honestly. "In fact, to be frank, Mr Winters, we're already bursting at the seams."

Eva sighed as the voices faded. She stroked Guinevere's neck. "You hear that? Mr Winters is checking up on us to see if we're too noisy."

Guinevere dipped her head and snorted.

"Exactly!" Eva agreed. "That's what I think. And Merlin thinks so too!" She pressed her lips together and made a "puh" sound. *Too noisy? What a load of rubbish!*

Eva caught sight of Mr Winters again on his way out. As she came out of the stables, he was shaking hands with her mum, but his face gave nothing away. Was he happy with what he'd seen, or not?

Heidi sighed and shook her head as she turned and walked back into the surgery. Eva was about to follow when she saw Linda Brooks greet Mr Winters on the pavement.

"Ah, Mr Winters!" she called. "I'm glad you followed up my letter of complaint and my petition. Now you can see for yourself how difficult it is for the residents of Okeham to have this animal rescue centre in our midst!"

Mr Winters's reply was too low for Eva to hear, but as she stood watching, Jason Brooks's car pulled into the drive next door and Annie jumped out of the car.

"Hey, Eva!" Annie cried, dumping her holiday bag and running into the yard. "Wow, am I glad to be back! How are you? What's new at Animal Magic?"

"Annie, come and say hi to your mum!"
Jason Brooks called in vain. He hurried
over to his wife's side just as Mr Winters
escaped Linda Brooks's clutches and
drove off.

Annie looked tanned. Her usually neat
hair was flying in all directions.

"How was Devon?" Eva asked.

"Cool. I rode ponies and swam in the
sea every day. But what's happening
here? What's with the long face?"

"That was only a visit from the Council
to see if your mum can get us closed
down!" Eva muttered. But she couldn't
stay glum for long. "Never mind, it's not
your fault, Annie. And guess what –
we've got a new foal. Come and look!"

"Annie!" Jason Brooks called after her.

"I won't be long!" she yelled as Eva
dragged her into the stables.

"Aah!" Annie's eyes lit up when she saw Merlin.

He was nestled in the deep straw, his long legs folded beneath him. He looked up at the two girls and blinked sleepily.

"How cute is he!" Annie breathed. "Can I go in and stroke him?"

Eva nodded. She led Annie into the stall. "Is this OK?" she asked Guinevere, who hovered close to where her foal lay.

The mare lowered her head and made way for Eva and Annie.

Annie knelt down next to Merlin and reached out to stroke him. "He's so soft!"

"He can stand and walk already!" Eva said, kneeling next to Annie.

Annie could hardly speak through her broad smile. "What's his name?"

"Merlin," Eva whispered.

Annie gave a soft laugh as Merlin nuzzled her hand. "And what's he doing here at Animal Magic?" she asked.

"He and his mum need a new home," Eva explained. "Hey, I don't suppose you know anyone who lives in a house surrounded by fields – someone who loves horses and has space to take in two more?"

Annie sat back. She thought for a while then answered, "Actually, Eva – I do!"

Chapter Six

"Devon?" Karl asked.

The family was discussing Guinevere and Merlin's future over supper that night. Eva had told them about Annie's pony-loving cousins by the sea.

"I know. It's miles away," Eva said. "But Annie's sure her aunty and uncle would take them. They already own a horse and a pony. And they have loads of space."

"But we'd never see them again," Karl pointed out.

"What's the family's name?" their dad asked thoughtfully.

Eva recalled the details that Annie had given her. "Simmons. There's her Aunty Ruth and Uncle David, plus Annie's two cousins, Jess and Molly. They live on a farm overlooking the sea."

"So that must be Linda's sister and her husband." Heidi worked it out as she collected the dirty dishes and put them in the dishwasher.

Eva traced patterns on the tablecloth with a spare fork. "What do you think, Mum? Is it a good idea?"

Heidi turned to Karl. "Have we had any replies to the advert on the website?"

He shook his head. "But it's only been up there for a day. Anyway, I think we should say no to Annie's idea – Devon is too far away."

"I know how you feel, but I think we should check it out," his dad argued. "Look at it from Guinevere and Merlin's point of view – a home by the seaside with other horses – it sounds perfect!"

"What else did Annie say?" Heidi asked Eva.

"She said her Aunty Ruth and her mum used to ride all the time when they were kids. Ruth is still a real animal lover, and Jess and Molly are too." Reluctantly Eva spoke the truth. Like Karl, she longed to find somewhere closer for Guinevere and Merlin.

Frowning moodily, Karl stood up from the table. "It's a stupid idea. What will Miss Eliot say? She'll have to say goodbye to Guinevere and never see her again. That's not fair!"

"Right!" Eva agreed, sorely regretting

that she'd mentioned the Devon thing. She looked from her mum to her dad, then back again.

"We need to talk to Miss Eliot," Mark pointed out. "After all, it will be her decision in the end."

"Meanwhile I'll call Leebank Pony Sanctuary and arrange a visit," Heidi said. "You never know – perhaps they'll have room for a mare and foal."

"I'll come!" Eva cried, grabbing on to her mum's new idea.

"Me too!" Karl volunteered.

Please let it be Leebank, not Devon! Eva wished as she left the house and made a beeline for the stables. *Better still, let it be Animal Magic for ever!*

How cool would that be! Guinevere and Merlin could live in Tom Ingleby's field at the back of their rescue centre.

And every morning Eva would get up and go down to the field to see the dapple-grey mare and her gorgeous foal. They would look up at her and whinny. She would greet them and they would trot through the lush green grass towards her.

Hey, she would even buy a saddle for Guinevere and learn to ride. Merlin would tag along until he was old enough to be schooled…

But in her heart Eva knew it wouldn't happen that way. No – Animal Magic would find a new home for the gorgeous duo and Eva's dream would end.

"Merlin is a newborn – he's just one day old," Heidi explained to Cath Brown, the owner of Leebank Pony Sanctuary the following morning. "We need to find a new home for him. Of course, we won't move him anywhere until he's a good deal older."

"Quite right." Cath nodded. "And you'll need to find someone who will keep him with his mother for the first year or so, until he's weaned and ready to leave her."

Eva and Karl sat in the back of their mum's car, listening to the grown-ups talk. "I like it here!" Eva muttered.

Karl grunted. He didn't dare to hope that Leebank would become Guinevere and Merlin's new home – that would be too good to be true.

"No, honestly – look at all the horses and ponies in the fields!"

Leebank sat in a valley with a stream running through it. The yard overlooked three big fields full of grazing animals.

"Fifteen – sixteen – seventeen," Karl counted. "...Twenty-two altogether."

Meanwhile Eva concentrated on Cath Brown, a tall, sturdy woman dressed in a blue padded jacket, jeans and wellies.

"I'm very happy to set up a link with Animal Magic," Cath was telling Heidi. "For instance, if people bring horses and ponies to me who are in need of a vet, I can bring them over to you for treatment. Likewise, if you need to rehome a pony and you've tried everywhere else without success, then I can provide a home here as a last resort."

"Look at that big brown and white one!" Karl nudged Eva and pointed to a horse that had come up to the gate.

Eva couldn't resist – she got out of the car and went to stroke the horse. He had thick, feathered legs and a long white mane that fell forward over his face. He was so hairy he even had a funny, curled moustache at the end of his nose.

"What's his name?" Eva called to Cath.

"That's Major. He's thirty-three years old." Cath came across with a carrot for the elderly horse.

"Wow!" Eva couldn't get over Major's size and hairiness. "What do you think about Guinevere and Merlin?" she asked.

Cath smiled. "They sound great. And

Guinevere sounds as if she's taken to motherhood, no problem."

"Merlin is so gorgeous!" Eva told her.

"And you're longing to keep him?" Cath guessed.

Major's moustache wobbled up and down as he ate his carrot.

"Yeah, but we can't," Eva sighed, enjoying the sight of other ponies ambling up the fields towards them. "Can you?" she asked suddenly, keeping her fingers crossed behind her back.

Cath sighed. "Like I said, Leebank is a last resort. And your mum says there's a chance of Guinevere and Merlin being sent to a good home in Devon."

"Miles and miles away!" Eva protested.

"But they would do well there – on a farm, with other animals, and kids to ride them."

"*I* could ride them if they lived here,"
Eva pleaded. She felt her hopes fade as
Cath smiled sympathetically.

"Send them to Devon," Cath advised.
"They'll have a good life down there."

Chapter Seven

"OK, so we have two people interested in Guinevere." As soon as they got back from the pony sanctuary, Karl went into Reception and checked the website. "One says she can't take Merlin though."

"We can't split them!" Eva insisted, reading the emails over her brother's shoulder. "And look, this other one's the opposite – they want the foal but not the mare. What's wrong with them? Don't they read the ads properly?"

"Hi, Annie, any news from Devon?" Heidi asked, looking up from her examination of Bruno as Eva's friend appeared. Late morning surgery had ended and all was quiet at Animal Magic.

"Aunty Ruth says she'll definitely think about giving Guinevere and Merlin a home," Annie replied cautiously, just as the phone began to ring. "But she can't give an answer right away."

Eva frowned. Right now, with Leebank only to be used as a last resort and no other offers coming up, Devon looked like the only choice.

"Answer the phone, would you, Eva?" Heidi muttered as she checked out movement in Bruno's injured shoulder.

Eva reached for the receiver.

"Hi, this is Cath Brown from Leebank," the voice said. "Is that Eva?"

"Yes, do you want to speak to Mum?"

"No. Can you just pass on a quick message? I forgot to mention one important thing when you dropped by, which is that the police called in here about a week ago to warn me that two horse thieves are operating in the area. I thought you should know, since it'll soon be time to put your mare and foal out to pasture. When you do, make sure the field is secure."

"OK, thanks." The message worried Eva. For a moment she wondered if the two angry fishermen she'd seen while walking Dougal had anything to do with the horse thieves. But when she told her mum, Heidi had good news.

"Don't worry, your dad fixed up a deal with Tom Ingleby earlier today. Tom has promised to rent us his field facing on to the golf course for as long as we need it. You know, the one you can see from your house, Annie."

"Hey, cool!" Annie grinned. "I'll be able to look out of my bedroom window and see Guinevere and Merlin!"

"So?" Eva prompted her mum, trying not to feel jealous.

"So, there's no direct access to that field from the main road," Heidi explained. "In other words, no horse thief can drive a trailer anywhere near Guinevere and Merlin when we put them out there tomorrow morning."

Reassured, Eva went off with Annie to feed the orphan kittens in the cattery. As they passed by Tigger's bay, Miss Eliot's tabby gave a loud miaow.

"What a gorgeous cat!" Annie said.

"He's going back to his owner as soon

as she's out of hospital, so don't get any ideas about adopting him," Eva kidded.

Annie sighed. "As if! You know what Mum's like!"

"I sure do!" Eva raised her eyebrows. Soon she and Annie were busy with the four tiny kittens, dropping milk into their greedy pink mouths.

The kittens squirmed and swallowed, curling their tongues around the plastic tube and sucking out every drop.

"So, you get to see Merlin out of your window and I don't," Eva sighed. Her bedroom overlooked the yard and the surgery.

"Yeah, but you got to see him being born!" Annie reminded her. "And you can stroke him whenever you like! I can't believe he feels so soft!"

"As soft as these kittens," Eva said. They were finished with the feeding and so she and Annie nestled the orphans down in their warm bed and left the cattery. "Do you fancy taking a peek at Merlin before you go?" she asked.

Annie glanced at her watch. "I promised Mum I'd be back for one – but hey, she won't mind if I'm a few minutes late!"

Eva led the way into the stables. "Hush!" she murmured, raising a finger to her lips.

Merlin was resting in the straw. Guinevere raised her head as the girls drew close and peered into the stall.

"Oh, he's so cool!" Annie breathed. "And skinny! And cute!"

Eva nodded happily. "Can we come in?" she asked Guinevere, gently opening the door and beckoning Annie in after her. "The first thing I thought after he was born was, 'Wow, how skinny!'" she confessed. "Then I saw him stand up on these long, wobbly legs, and I thought he'd never be able to do it, but Guinevere nudged him and he got up and he stood there trembling all over!"

"Is it OK to stroke him again?" Annie checked. "Oh, he's so gorgeous! Look, he's standing up!"

Jerkily getting to his feet, Merlin shook himself, and then tottered towards Eva.

He pushed his soft nose against her arm, and then gave a small hop and skip towards Annie.

"He likes me!" Annie smiled. But just as she reached out to stroke him, she heard her mother's voice calling and drawing nearer. "Uh-oh, I might have known!" With a start she drew back, making Guinevere glance anxiously towards the stable door.

"Annie, where are you? I warned you not to be late for lunch," Linda Brooks called.

"In here, Mum!" Annie replied softly, wiping her hands on her jeans as she backed out of the stall.

Linda appeared in the door, her forehead creased by a deep frown. But when she spotted Guinevere and her tiny foal, for a moment her face softened.

"Oh my!" she murmured, before the hard mask returned. She cleared her throat. "Annie, come along, your lunch is getting cold!"

Blushing, Annie joined her mum, who sneaked one final look at Merlin before she turned and marched away.

"Did you see that?" Eva muttered as she patted Guinevere's neck. "For a second back there I thought Mrs Brooks was about to crack a smile!"

The grey mare nuzzled at Eva's pockets.

"Sorry, no treats!" Eva smiled. "But listen, Guinnie, there was this look on Annie's mum's face, all soft and gooey, like everyone else when they first set eyes on Merlin. I was so surprised!"

This really made Eva think. She knelt down in the straw beside the foal, who cosied up for a stroke. "Of course, she soon switched it off, but I did see it. And you know something?" she murmured, wrapping her arms around Merlin's neck. "The truth is Linda Brooks fell in love with you on the spot."

Merlin turned his head and nuzzled Eva's shoulder.

Eva smiled. "She did," she insisted. "And you know something else? I've just had a totally brilliant idea!"

Chapter Eight

"Forget Devon!" Eva told Karl, brimming with confidence as she hurtled into his room.

Her brother was busy as usual updating the website. He sat with his back to her. "Sugar and Spice are orphan kittens," he typed. "They're ready to go to new owners and would like to find a home together."

"I said, forget Devon for Guinevere and Merlin!" Eva insisted. "I've thought of something brilliant!"

"So impress me," Karl muttered, scanning in an image of the two black kittens.

"I'm serious, Karl!" Eva swivelled his chair away from his desk. "Listen, you'd like to find Merlin and Guinnie a home close to Okeham, wouldn't you?"

"It's not up to us," he said. "Everyone else thinks Devon is a good idea."

"Except Miss Eliot!" Eva pointed out. "No one's told her yet, have they? It's going to break her heart!"

Karl frowned. "You're only saying that because you want to keep them nearby so *you* can see them!"

"No, I'm not."

"Yes, you are."

"Well, maybe a little, but do you want to hear my idea, or don't you?"

Karl turned back towards the screen.

"Go ahead. You're going to tell me anyway."

"OK, this is it! Mrs Brooks came to fetch Annie earlier and she saw Merlin..."

"Sage and Thyme," Karl typed, his shoulders hunched, his back to Eva again. "Two more orphan kittens looking for a friendly new home..."

"Her face softened the moment she saw him!"

"So?"

"So, she's like everyone else – she's fallen in love with him!"

"So?" Karl muttered again.

"So, she used to go riding when she was young – Annie told me. She loves horses, even if she tries to pretend she doesn't!"

"Are we talking about 'Linda Brooks', as in the woman who just sent a petition

to the Council to get us closed down?"
Karl scoffed.

"Karl, listen. You didn't see her face
when she set eyes on Merlin. She really
liked him. So my idea is to get Linda to
adopt him and Guinevere!"

Karl spun round in his seat, his eyes
narrowed. "You're crazy!"

"I'm not!"

"Yes, you are. You're always having mad ideas. Now let me get on, OK?"

Eva gritted her teeth. "You wait!" she muttered, flouncing off to her own room. "I'm going to make it happen!"

Next morning, Eva was bringing Joey the greyhound back from a walk by the river when she bumped into Annie at the entrance to Animal Magic.

"Hey, Eva, I was looking for you," Annie greeted her, stooping to pat Joey. "I've got good news. Mum spoke to Aunty Ruth again about Guinevere and Merlin and the answer's yes!"

"Oh!" Eva walked on towards the kennels with Joey.

"Aren't you pleased?" Annie ran after her. "Isn't that what you wanted?"

Just then, Eva's grandad drove through the gates and Karl came out of the house to say hello.

"How are my favourite grandkids?" Jimmy asked with a broad grin as he got out of his car.

"Grandad, we're your *only* grandkids!" Eva grinned back, handing Joey's lead to Annie, who had offered to put him back in his kennel.

"Exactly!" He gave her shoulder a quick squeeze. "I thought I'd come and check up on Tigger for Miss Eliot."

"How is she?" Karl asked.

"Not too bad. She comes out of hospital on Monday, into a flat with a warden to keep an eye on her. The old house is already up for sale."

"Well, tell her Tigger's fine," Karl said. "And we're pretty sure we've found a home for Guinevere and Merlin – in Devon."

"Yes, it's all fixed!" Annie announced, coming out on to the kennel porch.

Eva pressed her lips together and kept quiet, watching her grandad's reaction.

"Well, that's a long way away," Jimmy said, shaking his head. "I'm not sure how Miss Eliot will feel about that."

"She'll hate it!" Eva broke in.

"But it's a good home," Annie insisted.

"I'd better tell Miss Eliot then. I hope it doesn't come as too much of a shock," Jimmy said, worried. He set off for the house to find Mark and Heidi.

Eva ran after him. "Don't tell Miss Eliot about Devon just yet," she pleaded.

Her grandad turned to study her face. "Why? Have you got something else in mind?" he asked.

Eva's eyes were bright and eager. "Actually, yes!" she nodded. "I'm working on it. So don't worry, Grandad, I'm pretty sure I'll find Merlin and Guinevere a place *much* closer to home!"

"Meanwhile, it's business as usual," Heidi announced after she and Mark had finished telling Jimmy about the problem with the Council over a cup of coffee. Eva sat quietly in a corner of the kitchen, listening to their conversation.

"Did they say how long they'd take to make a decision?" Jimmy asked.

Mark shook his head. "But you know us, Dad – we always look on the bright side. There are lots of people in Okeham who support Animal Magic, in spite of the ones who signed Linda's petition.

"Why can't people like Linda Brooks see what a good job you're doing here?" Jimmy grumbled.

"Listen, we're not solving anything sitting here talking," Heidi decided, catching Eva's eye. "It's time to take Guinevere and Merlin out into the field for the first time. Eva, do you fancy putting a head collar on Guinevere and helping me lead her out?"

The words were hardly out of her mum's mouth before Eva was halfway across the yard. She dashed into the stables.

"Guess what!" she told Guinevere, grabbing a head collar from its hook on the wall. "You're going outside!"

The mare stamped her feet and turned to edge Merlin towards the door.

Carefully Eva strapped the head collar on and clipped a lead rope in place.

"Merlin, this will be the first time you've ever seen the sky and grass and a river ... and everything!"

The little grey foal gave a jerky hop, straight up in the air.

"Ready?" Heidi asked, appearing at the door. Behind her, Mark, Karl and Jimmy held back, curious to see how the new foal would enjoy going out into the field. "Do you want to lead the way?"

Heidi opened the door of the stall and they all made way for Eva and Guinevere. Little Merlin tottered close behind.

Eva led the procession across the yard and out through a side gate, down a narrow, leafy lane and into Tom Ingleby's field. Guinevere walked steadily, stopping to snatch a mouthful of fresh green shoots growing in the hedge. Close behind her, Merlin sniffed and trotted along.

At last they reached the field. Heidi opened the gate and Eva stepped in with Guinevere and Merlin.

The tiny foal took his first step on to lush green grass. He stayed close to his mother at first, following her every step.

Then Merlin grew braver. He moved away, taking a sniff here and a sniff there. He looked up at the vast blue sky. He tried out a small skip and a jump.

Guinevere kept a wary eye on him as he ventured out into the big wide world.

Hey, I can jump and I can run! Merlin seemed to say. *My legs are like springs! The air smells fresh and good!*

"Look at that!" Eva murmured, sitting astride the gate as Merlin made another run and a jump. He toppled and fell to the ground, got up again and trotted back to his mum.

"Adorable!" Heidi sighed.

Karl, Mark and Jimmy leaned against the gate grinning.

Eva watched Guinevere check that Merlin was OK before letting him go off to explore again. Then she glanced at the houses overlooking the field. She made out the back of the surgery, with its low roof and small windows, and next to it, the Brookses' tall, white house.

"Look, he's getting braver!" Karl exclaimed, as Merlin made his unsteady way up the hill, away from the river towards the houses.

Eva saw the curtain move in a window of the Brookses' house. She glimpsed Linda Brooks's face.

Yes! she thought. *Mrs Brooks is secretly watching! I knew it. I don't care what Karl says, my plan is going to work!*

Chapter Nine

"Hey, Eva, guess what!" It was Wednesday evening and Annie came looking for her friend in the cattery. "I just caught Mum sneaking a peek at Merlin when she should have been doing the hoovering!"

Eva gave a broad smile as she tucked Spice back into the basket alongside her brothers and sisters. "Tell me more."

"Mum was upstairs hoovering the bedrooms. I was downstairs and I heard everything go quiet. So I snuck up and found her standing at the window, just staring at Merlin in the field."

"Cool, it's working!" Eva grinned. She decided it was time to let Annie in on her plan. "Listen – my idea is to find a home for Guinevere and Merlin really nearby. I know your Aunty Ruth would take them, but I was thinking of somewhere *much* nearer than Devon."

"How much nearer?" Annie interrupted.

"So near that they wouldn't have to move at all!" Eva grinned. "My idea is to get your mum to fall in love with Merlin so she'll want to adopt him and his mum."

"When did you think of that?" Annie gasped.

"A few days ago. It was you who gave me the idea – when you said that your mum used to love ponies when she was a child."

"Yeah, I know, but..." Annie shrugged. "I guess it might work. But Aunty Ruth's already said yes and Mum's not the sort to back down easily. Remember how she feels about Animal Magic."

"Come into the stables and help me muck out," Eva suggested, guiding Annie across the yard. "People change their minds," she pointed out, sticking a spade into Annie's hands. She grinned again at the idea of Linda Brooks gazing down at the little grey foal during this, his fourth day in the sunny field. "And now that you know the plan, Annie, you have to work on your mum."

"How?"

"Tell her about Miss Eliot never seeing Guinnie again if she goes to Devon. Remind her how gorgeous ponies are, how much you'd like to have one because then you could learn to ride like she did when she was younger – all that kind of stuff."

Spade in hand, Annie promised to try. "But don't hold your breath," she warned.

"Try!" Eva insisted, finishing the work in the stable and picking up Guinevere's head collar. "Time to bring them in from the field. Do you want to come?"

Together the girls left the yard by the side gate and went down the footpath.

Everything was calm and quiet as usual, until Eva heard the sound of a car engine in the distance. "That's weird," she muttered, hurrying to the gate and spotting Guinevere and Merlin at the far side of the field.

Annie ran after her. "What is?"

"There's no way in for traffic, but I'm sure I just heard a car."

Sure enough, as she climbed the gate into Tom Ingleby's field, Eva saw a Land Rover and trailer crossing the old stone bridge over the river. It had driven straight across the empty golf course, heading for the ponies' field.

"That's not right!" she whispered, as alarm bells began to ring in her head.

Hadn't Cath Brown warned them about horse thieves in the area? And hadn't she herself seen two angry strangers

supposedly fishing on the river bank?
"Oh no!" she cried, setting off at a run.
She had a vision of the two men loading
Guinevere and Merlin into their trailer
and driving off at top speed.

To Eva's surprise, she wasn't the first
person to have spotted the Land Rover.
Linda Brooks had climbed her garden
fence and was sprinting down the field
towards the bridge.

The Land Rover towed the trailer over the bridge into the field.

"Stop!" Linda called. "This is private property. Leave the pony and her foal alone!"

Frightened by the disturbance, Guinevere and Merlin cantered off to the furthest corner of the field.

"They're horse thieves," Eva cried, beginning to panic. "We'll have to try and catch Guinevere!" She ran across the field determined to beat the thieves to it, hoping that the sight of Linda Brooks waving her arms and yelling would be enough to make them turn around.

"Mum, stop them. They've come to steal the ponies!" Annie cried.

The Land Rover came to a halt and two burly men stepped out.

"Turn around or I'll call the police!"

Linda insisted, going right up to the men. "You have no business to be here. The golf course is private, and this field is most certainly not a right of way!"

The men folded their arms and stood with their feet wide apart, taking in the panicky scene.

"Hey, Guinnie, it's OK," Eva said softly as she approached the mare. At her side, little Merlin trembled and peered out from behind her. "We won't let anything bad happen." Slowly she slipped the head collar on.

Meanwhile, Linda stood her ground. "Didn't you hear me? I said I'll call the police."

"And tell them what?" one of the men asked, the corners of his mouth twitching as he tried not to smile. "That Tom Ingleby sent us to set up some electric fencing?"

Linda stared. "Tom Ingleby?" she echoed.

The man nodded. "He's our boss. The fence posts are in the trailer if you'd like to check it out."

"Fence posts?" Taking a deep breath, Linda walked around the back of the trailer and peered inside. "Hmm," she muttered. "I thought ... I mean ... I was watching from my window ... I thought you were trespassing. And the girls here – they said you were horse thieves!"

"You can't be too careful," the man agreed. "I'm Dan Shaw. And this is Nathan. Nathan, get on to the boss on your mobile and get him to tell Mrs..."

"...Brooks," Linda mumbled. She was red and hot, her fair hair stuck to her forehead.

"Get him to tell Mrs Brooks that we are who we say we are."

"That won't be necessary," Linda
stammered, calling to Annie and Eva that
everything was OK. "I'm awfully sorry, Mr
Shaw. You must think I'm a total idiot!"

Slowly Eva led Guinevere and Merlin
towards the men with the trailer. Merlin
trotted calmly beside Annie.

Dan Shaw grinned. "I pity any poor
horse thief who tries to steal those two.
With you three around, they wouldn't
stand a chance!"

Linda's blushes deepened. "Annie, Eva, meet Dan and Nathan. They work for Tom Ingleby."

Eva gulped. Annie groaned. But the two men chuckled and said they would come back to do the fencing some other time, when the field was empty. Then they climbed into the Land Rover and drove slowly away.

"Oh wow!" Eva muttered and shook her head.

At his mother's side, Merlin suddenly took a little skip and hop towards Linda.

"Aah!" Annie sighed.

As Eva looked on quietly, she noticed Karl dashing across the field towards them.

"What happened?" he called. "How come Tom's men drove off without doing their job?"

Eva, Annie and Linda stared at him.

"You knew about Dan and Nathan?" Eva stammered.

Karl nodded. "I took a phone call from Tom Ingleby earlier this afternoon. He said to expect his men to turn up to set up some electric fencing."

"Thanks for telling us!" Eva groaned.

"Uh-oh, why do I get the feeling that my little sis just jumped to the wrong conclusion as usual?" Karl laughed.

"I'm afraid we all did," Linda confessed. She stroked Merlin and smiled as he hopped a little closer. Then he stuck out his nose and nuzzled her hand.

"Oh, how dreadful it would have been if those men really had been horse thieves!" Linda sighed. Gently she stroked the foal's soft nose. She went down on her knees and rested her cheek against his neck. "You're beautiful!" she whispered.

"I'm sorry if we scared you, but I thought those men were coming to steal you, and I couldn't let that happen!"

Annie nodded at Eva, who smiled back.

"You're totally gorgeous!" Linda murmured. She looked up at Eva with a tearful face. "What's his name?"

"Merlin," Eva replied.

"Like the wizard," Linda whispered. "Well, Merlin, you've worked your magic on me!"

Chapter Ten

"So you see, we think it would be a wonderful idea if Guinevere and Merlin could stay in Okeham," Linda Brooks told Heidi and Mark.

She'd called at the house with Annie late on Wednesday evening, just as Jimmy Harrison had arrived with Miss Eliot to pick up Tigger.

The farmhouse kitchen was full of visitors, all drinking tea around the big pine table. Annie sat beside Eva and Karl with an enormous grin on her face.

Mark cleared his throat. "Let me get this straight, Linda. Are you actually offering a home to the pony and her foal?"

Linda nodded. "I've talked with my sister, Ruth, on the phone, and she agrees it's by far the best solution to keep them here. I've also spoken to Tom Ingleby, who's perfectly happy to carry on renting us the field at the back of our house. And of course Jason agrees that it will be lovely for Annie to have a pony."

"Whoa!" Mark muttered, holding up both hands. "Did I miss something?" he whispered to Eva.

The shock waves of Linda's offer allowed Miss Eliot to break into the conversation. "Oh it would be wonderful to be able to visit Guinevere!" she sighed. "It softens the blow of having to sell Ash

Tree Manor if I know I can still see my beautiful pony!"

"And her new foal!" Eva added. She had a warm glow in her stomach, knowing that Animal Magic had once more done its work to match the perfect pet with the perfect owner.

"Well, Annie, there's no need to ask how you feel about the arrangement!" Heidi smiled. "I can tell by the look on your face that you think you're in heaven."

"Pinch me, someone!" Annie sighed. "I'm actually going to have my own pony. Eva, because this is all down to you, you can ride Guinevere whenever you want!"

"Now someone has to pinch me and make me believe what's happening!" Eva exclaimed, closing her eyes and picturing herself riding Guinnie by the river, with Merlin trotting along at their side.

Heidi turned back to Linda. "And does this mean you'll be withdrawing your petition to have us closed down?"

An embarrassed frown appeared on Linda's face. "I'm afraid it's too late for that. Mr Winters tells me that he's in the middle of writing his report."

"So we'll have to wait and see." Mark nodded.

"Oh dear, oh dear," Miss Eliot said softly. "I had no idea!"

"Come and see Merlin?" Eva cut in, eager to change the subject. She, Annie and Karl led the old lady out to the stables. The grown-ups followed behind.

There, in the glow of the lamp, Guinevere stood guard over her foal. She raised her head and snickered as Miss Eliot approached.

"Who's my clever girl!" the old lady sighed, gazing down at Merlin. "What a beautiful little creature you are!"

Merlin looked up from his bed of straw. He was too sleepy to get up, though he raised his head and flicked his ears towards the visitors.

"Wonderful!" Miss Eliot murmured with tears in her eyes.

Karl stood with his hands in his pockets, doing the don't-show-your-emotions boy thing. But Eva felt her own tears well up. Guinevere and Merlin would never be more than a stone's throw from Animal Magic. It was a dream come true.

Annie couldn't help it – she cried in full view of everyone. "I'm just so-o-o happy!" she sniffed.

And Merlin settled down in his warm bed and slept.

Look out for the next book in the series!

Rusty

The injured fox cub

Everyone enjoys having Rusty the fox cub to stay at Animal Magic, especially Eva, who can't help treating him as a pet. Eva knows that the cub must be returned to the wild, but has her love and care ruined Rusty's chances of being set free?